REYNARD THE FOX

AND OTHER FABLES

Adapted from the French of
Jean de La Fontaine

Retold by
Will Trowbridge Larned

Illustrated by
John Rae

DOVER PUBLICATIONS, INC.
Mineola, New York

Bibliographical Note

This Dover edition, first published in 2014, is an unabridged republication of the work originally published by The P. F. Volland Company, Joliet, Illinois, in 1925.

Library of Congress Cataloging-in-Publication Data

Larned, W. T. (William Trowbridge)
    Reynard the fox and other fables / adapted from the French of Jean de La Fontaine ; retold by Will Trowbridge Larned ; illustrated by John Rae.
        pages cm
    "This Dover edition, first published in 2014, is an unabridged republication of the work originally published by The P. F. Volland Company, Joliet, Illinois, in 1925."
    Summary: A collection of eighteen fables as told by Jean de La Fontaine, including "The Tortoise Who Ran a Race with the Hare" and "The Grapes Hang High for Reynard the Fox."
    ISBN-13: 978-0-486-78197-6
    ISBN-10: 0-486-78197-6
    1. Fables, French—Adaptations. [1. Fables.] I. Rae, John, 1882–1963, illustrator. II. La Fontaine, Jean de, 1621–1695. III. Aesop. IV. Title.
PZ8.2.L326Re 2014
398.2—dc23
                                                             2014011974

Manufactured in the United States by Courier Corporation
78197601   2014
www.doverpublications.com

HOW REYNARD THE FOX FOOLED THE RAVEN

SOME folks say, Reynard the Fox is a rascal. They will tell you he is sly, and up to all sorts of tricks. He prowls around at night, smelling the air with his long nose, and listening with his long ears; and when he has done prowling, you may be pretty sure he is not as hungry as when he set out.

If there are partridges to be had, he makes his meal on partridges. No one — not even you or me — likes a fat bird better than the Fox likes it; the only difference being that *we* like the bird on toast, hot from the oven, and cooked just so, while the Fox is not nearly so fussy, and is quite content with his meal, only asking that there be enough!

But perhaps there *are* no partridges. Perhaps the human hunters, with dogs to aid them, have beaten up the woods so often, and shot so many with their shot-guns, that the birds have all flown away; so the next time the hungry man in a hotel says, "I think I'll take partridge on toast," the waiter with a white apron answers, "Sorry, sir; but the Foxes are very bad this year, and we are all out of partridges. But the roast beef is very good this evening." And then the hungry man looks cross, and eats his dinner so fast that it almost chokes him; and he blames the waiter, and blames the Foxes, and says the red rascals should all have been killed long ago.

7

And the hungry man in the hotel is not the only one who hates the Fox. Neither does the farmer love him much. When the Fox is hungrier than usual, and cannot find any game birds to eat because so many men with guns and dogs have tramped the woods up and down — why then Reynard the Fox will sometimes risk his life to steal a goose or a chicken from the farm; and if he is not taken in a trap, or hunted down with dogs, it is likely that he will come again some other night for another meal.

The fact is, the Fox may be as fussy about his meals as the hungry man in the hotel. If he can't have a partridge, he *must* have a chicken or a goose. But we *must* say this much for him: Oftener than not, he's content enough with whatever comes along. If the boys with *their* dogs have not frightened away all the rabbits, why a rabbit will do well enough. And if not a rabbit, a few fat mice will answer, or maybe a mess of worms or insects. But if these are scarce also, and he happens to live near the sea, he will take a stroll along the beach, and make his dinner on whatever crabs may come his way. And as for fruit — he always did have a weakness for grapes!

The Fox enjoys a joke — even a joke on himself. If you should frown at him and say: "Don't you know it's very, very wicked for *you* to eat birds!"— likely as not he'd wink, and reply without cracking a smile, "Well, we have to *live*, don't we?"

If the Fox is not popular with farmers, neither is he much beloved by some of the other animals. This has been the case ever since that time, long ago, before man himself was created — when the animals ruled the earth, and the lion was their lord and king. In fact, the Fox family was one of the first families we know anything about; as old as the great mammoth, that disappeared so long ago, leaving only a few bones for us to remember him by.

And the Fox family is not only old. It is celebrated. The name, Reynard, you must know, is a French name for the Fox; and the Fox was made famous in France by stories told about him long before books were printed. This story of the Fox was written by a number of French writers; and was not only one of the first stories written in France, but one of the most amusing and most popular. In these, and even earlier tales, the Fox is the hero. Sometimes — as when he tries to outwit Chanticleer, the Cock — he meets his equal in intelligence, and sometimes he is made to suffer. But the Wolf, though much stronger and more savage, is no match for the clever Fox; the big Bear is overcome by his cunning; the Lion himself is made a laughing stock; and all the little enemies of Reynard are put to rout

There is, you see, a good deal to be said in his favor. Were it not for his cunning, his ferocious old enemy, the Wolf, might have made away with him long ago; were he not so swift of foot, and were his sense of smell not so keen, the man with the gun would have shot him down. As it is, he outlives the Wolf. As it is, man must take him in traps when he wants his fur for winter garments; or must run him to earth on horseback, with a pack of dogs, when it is only his "brush," or tail, that is wanted for a "trophy."

Of all the wild animals he is one of the wildest, and loves his freedom dearly. He would rather run wild, and trust to his wits for a living, than suffer himself to be tamed and fed well in captivity. Bear cubs are caught, and grow up, and are taught to dance — though the dance is hardly a gay one; lions are tamed to jump through hoops, and to fear the whip and the goad. But you cannot tame the Fox. *His* cubs, too, have been caught, and kept for pets; but a pet Fox is a poor sort of thing. He does not like to be petted, or to eat from anyone's hand. You cannot teach him tricks, as you would teach a monkey. Tricks he knows a-plenty. But these are his own tricks, that he invented for himself, as a protection against his enemies, and are not at all the tricks that animals in cages or animals in chains are taught to do.

Whatever else he may be, Reynard is handsome and clever.

9

His handsomest coat is reddish brown above and white below, and the tip of his bushy tail is also white; while his cleverest trick is to double on his trail and deceive a whole pack of hounds yelping in close pursuit. Perhaps if he were only plain and a bit stupid, he would be better off. And because he *has* both brains and good looks, and was always envied, we are told, by some animals who have *neither*, you need not *wholly* believe everything you hear against him. In this book you are reading you will find four stories about the Fox. These were written a long time ago — like the other tales told here; but people are always wanting to hear them again; so here they are! The first is the story of the Raven who provided a meal for Reynard at the Raven's own expense.

ONCE there was a Fox who lived in a hole made by a Rabbit. It was an empty hole when the Fox found it for the Rabbit had been chased away by the hounds, and would never return. Reynard, however, was not much afraid of the hounds. Unless there was a large pack of them, trained in the chase, and urged on by men who rode horses, he had always been able to show them his heels in anything like a fair race for cover. So he scooped out the hole, to make it big enough for Mrs. Fox and the little Foxes, and settled down there for a time.

When the little Foxes were old enough to play around and chase their own tails, like so many kittens, but were not yet knowing enough to forage for themselves, Papa Reynard needed all his wits and all his time to get food for the family. It was at night that he did most of his hunting for at night the hounds were in their kennels, and some of the things he liked to eat best were then most easily obtained. But sometimes when he had trotted far and wide, and was on his way home, he had not found enough food for all. So he would nose around until the sun was well up; or perhaps return to his hole, and make a fresh start.

"You *are* a handsome bird."

One night he had had less luck than usual. The little Foxes gulped down almost all he had fetched — leaving only a bite or two for Mrs. Fox, and then opened their mouths for more. There was nothing for Papa Reynard to do but to try his luck again; so off he went.

Being pretty hungry himself by this time, a worm or a mouse was not to be despised; and when he came across a beetle — well, you may be sure that beetle could scarcely say, "Goodbye, brother insects!" before the Fox had gobbled him up. On he trotted — sometimes with his nose to the ground, and sometimes with his nose in the air. He did not mean to miss anything that crawled or anything that flew. And his hunger, instead of making him discouraged, had only sharpened his wits. It was a time for anything with wings or anything with legs, that would make a good mouthful or two, to look out and move quick.

Pretty soon he came to the edge of the woods. And here he sat up on his haunches and looked ahead; for the sun had risen, and his enemies were not so far away. He saw a stone wall, fencing a field with growing crops. Just beyond the wall was a thing that looked much like a man, with one hand grasping a stick and the other hand upraised. Reynard the Fox gave one look at it — and laughed.

"To think," he said to himself, "that any intelligent bird

or beast could be taken in by that old Scarecrow. Bah! No wonder that man considers himself the *superior* animal. But no *Fox*, I am glad to say, was ever fooled by a stick with an old hat on it! It couldn't even deceive a Crow."

No sooner had he said this than a flutter of wings was heard overhead; and down on the limb of a tree, and just a few feet away, settled a great black bird, with something that looked like a piece of cheese held firmly in its strong black beak. It was ever so much larger than a Crow. When its wings were spread wide they measured almost three feet from tip to tip; and even its feet and tongue were black.

Reynard recognized the Raven at once. It was a pet Raven, belonging to the Farmer in the house just beyond the field. There is nothing a Raven does not eat; and they do say he is not particular about asking first whether he may have it. Ten to one, he had stolen the cheese, and flown away with it where no one would see him.

"The black thief!" said the Fox. But he said this to himself. Then, in a loud voice, and suddenly, he remarked to the Raven:

"Good-day to you, and a good appetite!"

His hope was that the Raven would be startled, and drop the cheese; but the big bird's grip was too strong. The Raven knew Reynard's voice, and was not scared; but just nodded "Good-day!" without saying a word.

Reynard thought a while. "The black scoundrel!" he said again to himself. Reynard saw he was getting into a rage; and that would never do. Only stupid animals got angry; and what was the use of *that?* No use at all. So what he said was — and he said it in a voice of honey:

"You're getting younger and blacker every day, and *I* am getting grayer and older. However, I am thankful that I still see and hear well. Would you believe it, though, I just made an odd mistake — though not so odd when you come to think of it. I heard a Meadow Lark sing, and I stopped to listen. It was a lovely song — the notes so sweet and clear;

so inspiring. I was feeling a little blue, and the song really made me glad I was alive. But, say — what do you think? Now, don't suppose for a moment I'm flattering you. If there's anything I detest, it's flattery. But the fact is, at first I did not *know* it was a Meadow Lark. The voice was so pure, so — so *pianissimo*. That is the right word, is it not? Well, to make a long story short — I thought it was *you* who were singing."

The Raven is a solemn bird — serious as can be; with no ear at all for music. He cannot tell the choiring of a songbird from the quack of a Goose. But *he knows what he likes;* and what he likes most is, alas! the sound of his own voice. It is, to be sure, just a croak; but he does not know it. Somehow, no one had ever praised it before. But here was a critic who could *tell*. Sing? Why to be sure! This time his beak opened wide, and down fell the cheese — almost in the mouth of the Fox, who was standing straight up, with his forelegs against the trunk of the tree.

Reynard paused for one moment.

"Croak, croak!" sang the Raven.

Once more the Fox smiled.

"Such a voice!" said he. "Some day I'll come again. When I do, I'd like to hear you sing a duet. . . . . . *With a Jay!*"

He pounced upon the cheese, and carrying the choice morsel in his mouth, plunged into the woods and disappeared.

And all the Raven said was: "Nevermore!" What else *could* he say?

THE RAVEN WHO WOULD BE LIKE AN EAGLE

YOU will remember that when Reynard the Fox fooled the Raven, he recognized in that foolish bird one who had been caught by the farmer, who clipped his wings so he could not fly too far, and kept him for a pet. You thought no doubt that the Raven was rather silly to be taken in so easily. And he *was* silly — not only silly but vain; and so we did not feel sorry for him — especially as he was not a bit hungry and did not need the cheese, whereas the Fox and the little Foxes needed it badly.

But silly and vain as the Raven was when he thought he could sing, and so let go the food he carried in his beak, he was just as foolish and just as conceited when he did the stupid thing that enabled the farmer to catch him. The Raven is a bird that lives for many, many years; and he was old enough to know better when he came to grief this first time, and had his wings clipped by the farmer. But some birds, like some people we have met, do not grow wiser as they grow older — and all because they are *vain*, and try to do things that are quite beyond their power. Listen to this story of how the Raven believed himself the equal of the Eagle in strength; and then you can judge for yourself.

15

This farmer kept a flock of Sheep, who grazed high up on the hills, in a country where Eagles are often seen. The sheep loved it there and would climb higher and higher at the word of the Shepherd for the tender grasses and refreshing herbs that grew close to the sky. They liked the flowers that grew there, too—mountain flowers, every color. These Sheep were watched over by a shepherd with a crook — the same kind of crook that Little Bo-Peep carried when she lost her Sheep and didn't know where to find them. Little Bo-Peep was a lucky little girl. The rhyme says that if she left them alone, the Sheep would come home, and bring their tails behind them. Perhaps they did. Mother Goose does not say, and we can only hope that all turned out well.

But in this story things did *not* turn out so well. There was a Black Sheep in the flock, who was always setting a bad example to the others. He would wander off by himself; and the shepherd — who wore a Scotch plaid, as you can see by the picture — would have to send his shepherd dog after the Black Sheep, to bring him back safe to the flock. One day, when this Sheep had strayed off all alone — for no better reason in the world than because he thought he could take care of himself, an Eagle swooped down from the sky. He was so high up that the Shepherd Dog had not seen him; and when he did see him the mischief had been done. The Eagle seemed to be falling — so sudden and so swift was that terrible swoop. The Black Sheep bleated; the Shepherd Dog heard him, and ran like a streak to his aid. But it was too late. In a moment the powerful Eagle had fastened his crooked claws in the Sheep's woolly back, and was flying off to his nest.

This made the Shepherd more careful than ever. At least he was glad it was the Black Sheep — who would never trouble him again — and not one of the white Sheep; and he consoled himself by thinking it was not his fault or the fault of the Shepherd Dog, but entirely the fault of the Black Sheep, who had now paid dearly for his folly.

The Raven's claws
are caught, and stick.

All this time the Raven had been looking on, from his perch on a tall tree. He is a clumsy creature, and rather slow when you compare his flight with the flight of the Eagle or the Hawk; and being so awkward and so slow, and perhaps a little lazy besides, he generally made his meal on little young birds who could not well escape him. So not only the farmers, but the game-keepers as well, had little love for him; and Ravens were rather scarce.

This particular Raven was a great imitator. He tried to be everybody but himself. One day the Raven was watching the Shepherd Dog wag his tail.

The Raven tried one of the Shepherd Dog's wide, friendly wags and it threw him from the tree in an awkward flutter. Ravens are like that.

When the Raven saw the Eagle fly away with the Sheep, his dull wits began to work. "That Eagle," said he to himself, "gets his dinner pretty cheap. And such a dinner! Mutton chops, mutton pie — mutton everything! Mutton enough, and more than enough, to last *me* a month. What an idiot I am! Scratching for a living like a common Hen in a cornfield; hopping as hard as I can for a few skinny birds that hardly make a mouthful — while that big bully, the Eagle, takes one snatch at a Sheep, and gets away with it.

I'll show him! I reckon Ravens have their rights the same as that spotted old sky robber! Wish I thought of it first!"

As no one was at hand to answer his argument, he now felt sure he was equal to anything. All that remained was to pick out a good, fat sheep on the outer edge of the flock, watch his chance when the shepherd dog was not too near, and then — !

He was so excited he could hardly wait. Some little Lambs were frisking around, not far off; but the Raven had completely lost his head. Nothing would do for *him* but a big, fat Sheep — the bigger and fatter the better. Pretty soon a fat Sheep did come nibbling the grass in his neighborhood.

"Now or never!" croaked the Raven.

Down he flew, and fastened his claws in the Sheep's thick wool — just as the Eagle had done. Then he flapped his wings, and tried to fly away with it.

"Ba, ba!" cried the Sheep. "Hi, hi!" called the shepherd. "Bow — wow!" barked the Dog!

And now it was the Raven's turn.

"Caw, caw!" he screamed, as the shepherd and the Dog approached. "Caw, caw! Who would have thought this wretched animal was so heavy!"

In vain he tried to release himself, and fly away. His claws were caught fast in the thick wool; the more he struggled the faster he was caught.

"I've a good notion to wring your neck!" exclaimed the shepherd.

· Then he laughed. It was all so comical — enough to make the Dog laugh, too.

"I'll just take you home with me," said the shepherd on second thought. "Perhaps I can teach you to behave."

Any other bird caught like the Raven would have fretted and pined about being kept indoors and trained to fetch and carry. The Raven didn't mind it a bit. After he became thoroughly acquainted with the Shepherd and the Shepherd Dog he flew from one to the other taking food from their plates and pecking their hands and cawing like a spoiled child when they wouldn't let him have everything he wanted. When he became too great a bother the Shepherd Dog would bark at him and rumple his feathers until he would fly to a far corner of the room and sit quietly.

And so the Raven was spared — to sing for Reynard the Fox.

THE DOG WHO GOT A GOOD DUCKING

THE Raven no doubt was foolish when he tried to fly away with a Sheep; and certainly he was silly when he thought he could sing for the Fox. Yet, after all, even the educated among us make our little blunders; and the wisest of us sometimes do things at which the Raven himself might laugh.

The Dog, for example — as these are stories of animals. How intelligent he is, and how easily taught. Only a brute, to be sure, who must run along on four feet, while we have the use of two hands; but when he puts his *best* foot forward, it is time we did not hold our heads *quite* so high. As for what he will do for his master — *that* is too well known to talk about. In time of war and in time of peace, in time of plenty and in time of need, man can always count on his Dog.

The Dog is not up to mean tricks — which is one of many reasons why we love him. His tricks are playful and innocent; and sometimes he has been known to play tricks on himself! One trick that a Dog played on himself was played long, long ago. It taught him a lesson, and it taught others a lesson; and that is probably why it has never been forgotten, and is told again and again, so that other Dogs may take warning.

Pointer the Dog was a fine, handsome fellow — well bred and well brought up. Luckily for him, he lived in the country — the place where a Dog that *is* a Dog *ought* to live. There he could run and be happy — without a muzzle and without a leash; and so he was strong and healthy, and had the appetite of a Dog that is always running.

By the looks of his well-made collar you may judge that he had a good master; and by the looks of the bone he carried in his jaws you may believe it was juicy, with plenty of marrow, and that he trotted off to enjoy it — to crunch it awhile perhaps, and then bury it in a safe place.

He took a path he had seldom travelled before, and pretty soon he came to a stream, at a place where the water was dammed in a deep pool. How could he cross it? He made his way to the edge of the bank, where the trees were reflected in the smooth surface of the stream. It was like a looking glass.

What was it that he saw there? Another Dog — or so it seemed! A Dog the image of himself — the same size and color, and wearing a collar exactly like his own. What is more — this other Dog carried in his mouth a bone as big as the one *he* had. As big, and no doubt even better, he thought.

There he saw another one.

Now Pointer was the prize Dog of that neighborhood; and he did not like the idea of another Dog, just as big and handsome as himself, and with a better bone to crunch than *he* had. And these woods, where the strange Dog made so free, were his master's woods. What impudence! He would teach him a lesson, and take the bone for himself.

Splash! In he plunged. But what had become of the strange Dog; and what had become of the bone? Both had vanished. What is more, he had let go of his own bone; and that, too, had disappeared.

Dripping and disgusted, he swam to the bank, and just managed to crawl out — a sadder and let us hope, a wiser Dog. The next time he saw his shadow in the water, he would *know* it was only a shadow, and would think twice before he lost a bone in trying to get another that was not a bone at all!

THE TORTOISE WHO RAN A RACE WITH THE HARE

THOUGH Reynard the Fox is so swift that he often outruns the Hounds, he is not as swift as the Hare, whose long hindlegs enable him to take great leaps, and send him far ahead of almost anything with four feet. Even the Greyhound, with *his* long legs, is not always a match for the Hare; and with an open country and an equal chance, it is hard to say just which one would run the faster.

Suppose, then, we should say that a Tortoise once ran a race with a Hare — what would you think of *that?* It would perhaps seem to you as funny as it seemed to the Hare, when the Tortoise proposed the race that turned out to be the strangest sort of race ever run.

When you look at the picture of these two, it will make you wonder how such a thing could be possible. The Hare's long legs are tucked up under him, as he sits and listens to what the Tortoise has to say. If the Tortoise had never seen him except when he *was* sitting, with his hindlegs half-hidden — then perhaps you might understand. Surely the Tortoise did not expect to win a race with his *long neck*. His neck *is* much longer than the Hare's; so perhaps he thought that if the race was a close one, he could thrust it out, at the last moment, and thus *win by a neck* — as a horse sometimes beats another horse.

However this may have been, it is evident that the Hare could hardly believe his ears, though his ears seem to be the sort that are *made* to hear with. There he sits, listening to the Tortoise, with a fore-paw covering his mouth, and his body bent almost double. He looks as if he might be laughing *inside*, and that if the Tortoise keeps on, he will laugh out loud — or *split*.

The Tortoise, on the other hand, is entirely serious. There he sits, almost all shell — with queer little legs that one would say were made just for *crawling*, when not drawn up out of sight.

"I'll tell you how it is," he seems to be saying. "I'm not as young as I was, and not as spry on my feet. No one ever *saw* me run — that's true enough. But I *can* run, and I bet you I can beat you at it. Come on, I dare you!"

But the Hare was not so easily persuaded. It was by no means the first time he had heard this sort of talk from the Tortoise; and though he was amused by it to begin with, he began to grow impatient, and almost lost his temper.

"Pooh!" we can fancy him saying. "If you want to show somebody how you can run — there's the Beetle. *He's* a creature right in your class. *I'll* arrange the race, and act as umpire."

"That's all right," replied the Tortoise. "But you should have seen me catch a Centipede the other day; and he had a good start, too."

"Go chase *yourself!*" retorted the Hare, whose words were rather wild at times. "Go chase yourself, I say! Do you know what's the matter with *you?* You've had your head out too long in the sun, and the heat has affected your brain. Get back into your shell, and I'll fetch a Doctor. I saw old Doctor Crane down the creek, a bit ago. His *bill* is pretty long; but what's the difference if he *cures* you?"

"I'll run you a race,
if you dare."

The Hare thought his joke about the Crane's *bill* was one of the funniest things he had ever said. He was so pleased with it that he began to laugh. But the Tortoise never cracked a smile. The truth is, if you look hard at a Tortoise you will decide that whatever his fine points may be, a joke would be quite wasted on him. The Hare, however, did not mind that. He would tell the joke to Mrs. Hare and the Little Hares, and it would put them all in a good humor. That's the great advantage of a joke. Sooner or later, *somebody* is almost sure to see it, no matter how poor it is.

Then the Hare, because he felt so happy, suddenly changed his mind. Hares are *always* changing their minds.

"Come on!" said he. "I'll run you — just for a joke."

For a race-course the Tortoise selected an open place he knew well — free from stumps and stones. Some distance off was a sign-post; and whoever reached that first would be the winner.

"One, two, three," said the Tortoise. "Go!"

The Hare made a few leaps, and then paused to look over his shoulder. Away behind him was the Tortoise — so far behind he could scarcely be seen.

"This will never do," said the Hare. "It's too much like taking candy from a Cotton-tail. It's too *one-sided!* I'll just take a little nap, and wait for the Tortoise to come closer.'

He curled up and shut his eyes; and when he opened them again the Tortoise was nowhere to be seen.

"Here I am!" said a voice.

It was the voice of the Tortoise; and where do you suppose it came from? It came from behind the sign-post. The Tortoise had reached it first, and *won the race!*

"You see," said he to the Hare. "The race is not always to the swift; and it's just as important to get a good start."

"The race is not always to the swift!"

You will often hear this said; but the Tortoise said it first. No wonder that the words appear on the Tortoise coat-of-arms! Turn this page, and you can read them for yourself.

The Race is not always
to the Swift

HOW THE HIRED MAN LEARNED A LESSON

REUBEN the hired man had many good qualities and few bad ones. He always did as he was told, and did it cheerfully. His hours were long and his work was hard; but he did not complain. He knew how to sow, and how to reap. When he swung a scythe it was with a wide, sure sweep; and when he milked the kicking cow he got the last drop of milk. He could plow and he could pitch hay with the best of them; and no one knew so well how to set the sheaves of grain together in a shock. The axe and the pitchfork, the hoe, the spade and the rake, were tools that came easy to his hand; and when he had used them he put them under cover, and never left them laying around in the rain.

Yes, Reuben earned his wages. No one could deny it.

The only thing the matter with Reuben was — he did not like to think! Thinking somehow tired him — tired him a great deal more than all the hard work he did with his powerful hands. When he plucked a goose his nimble fingers would make the feathers fly; but when he took a goose *quill* — which he used for a pen — and sat down to write a letter, it was quite another thing. To look at Reuben trying to

31

write a letter, you would think he was in great pain. He would sit all hunched up, as if he had the colic, and make queer motions with his tongue. Then he would stop and scratch his head awhile. Reuben would rather plow an acre of new land than write a few lines that always began with "Dear Friend," and always ended with: "Well, I must close now. Hoping this will find you the same."

However, it is just as well not to laugh too heartily at Reuben. If thinking made him tired, it was perhaps because he worked too hard with his hands, and with his whole body — doing so many useful things all day long that he was much too weary to use his mind.

And Reuben was no fool. Not by any means. In fact, when one comes to think of it, the lesson he learned from the acorn and the pumpkin was a lesson he taught himself, and therefore one he was sure always to remember.

It came about in this way: One day Reuben had been gathering pumpkins; and at noon he stopped to rest. Pausing for a moment under an oak tree, he idly plucked a twig laden with acorns, and stood there — looking at them, for no particular reason. Then his eyes wandered to the pumpkins, and an odd notion came into his head.

"Mighty queer," he said to himself, "the way these things grow. "There's that big, heavy pumpkin with a foolish little stem you can snap in two betwixt your finger and your thumb; and there's a big oak tree that might bear as many pumpkins as an apple-tree bears apples. Looks kind o' wasteful to me. All the strength in that tree goin' out into acorns, that might just as well be a-growin' on the ground, same as strawberries. Now, if *I* had had a hand in plannin' how these things should grow, the pumpkins would be hangin' from this tall oak, and the acorns would be ripenin' on the earth, fastened to the stem that holds the pumpkins. But it's just the other way aroun', and to save my life I can't see any sense in it."

Reuben yawned, and stretched his arms. So much hard thinking had made him tired. He looked again at the twig

32

"Gosh!" he said. "Suppose a pumpkin
Came a-fallin' on my face!"

laden with the acorns, and shook his head. Then, as the hour was noon, and he had earned a rest after using his muscles all morning, he stretched himself out under the tree.

It was a warm day, the sun was hot; and lying there in the shade, with nothing to do for a time, was a pleasant change. Pretty soon his eyes closed, the wrinkles of thought were smoothed from his honest face, and he lay there flat on his back, and fast asleep.

Then it was he dreamed a wonderful dream. He dreamed that he lived on a farm where everything grew as it ought to grow. The chickens laid eggs in season and out — they laid so many eggs he had all he could eat and sometimes enough left so when Rover licked the plate there was a speck there for him. The next part of his dream was true enough — the dog brought in the cows and horses and that was a great help. He was a good dog — the cows and horses liked him and didn't mind coming in when he came out to tell them it was six o'clock. Then there was the cat — there was only one new kitten and he could keep that instead of the usual dozen that would have to be taken all over the country before homes could be found for them. There were never any weeds or briars in the wheat, and no potato bugs on the potatoes. The earth he plowed was free from stones; it always rained at the right time; and never when he was getting in the hay. Then he remembered the pumpkins and the acorns. On a farm like this, where everything grew as it ought to grow, the pumpkins should be hanging from the oak tree and the acorns should be growing on the ground where they belonged.

"I'll just take a look," said Reuben in his dream; "and if it hasn't been changed for the better, then it's high time *I* took a hand, and set things right."

But just at that moment something happened. Something fell from a branch overhead. Plump! It was an acorn; and it hit the hired man full upon his nose.

Reuben awoke, and rose to his feet, just in time to see

the acorn bounce from his nose and roll away. He picked it up, and holding it between a finger and thumb, stood there scratching his head and looking down at the acorn as if he had seen it now for the first time.

Slowly it came into his head that he had been a fool, and that the ways of nature were much better than his ways.

"Gosh!" he said. "If that had been a pumpkin, 'stead of a acorn, I allow it would have smashed my nose out flat!"

Then he grinned and went back to his work. After all, Reuben could change his mind when he saw he was in the wrong; and that is more than *some* people can do.

THE HERON WHO WAS HARD TO PLEASE

ALBA, the great white Heron, stretched his long neck, opened and shut his long, sharp bill, flapped his beautiful wings — and looked out over the water. He was, as you may see by his picture, a rather important bird; and being both important and handsome, he had a certain dignity which he never quite forgot.

You could tell this by the way he walked. His movements were slow and deliberate. He would raise one leg carefully, as if considering how high he had better raise it; and then he would put it down and lift the other leg in the same stately manner.

Just now Alba was asking himself: "Am I hungry or am I *not* hungry?" And as no really hungry person ever asks himself such a question, we may conclude that Alba was *not*. This may seem strange for a Heron. But perhaps you have read the sign in a railway restaurant: "Meals at All Hours!" and then you will understand. *That* is the time that Alba ate his meals — *at all hours!*

It was almost *half* an hour since Alba had eaten some shellfish; so, instead of looking for more, he decided to go for a stroll instead. "Time enough," said he. "I'm a little tired of the fish I find in this creek. It's pike and carp, carp and pike, day in and day out. No variety at all. Besides, I like an edge to my appetite; and I find that if I wait a few minutes between meals, and am not *always* stuffing myself with whatever comes along, I enjoy it much better."

He glanced carelessly at the stream that provided him with food; and saw a great pike swimming slowly along.

"Pike again!" exclaimed the Heron. "Pooh! Now, if a golden carp came my way — but it would have to be a *golden* carp, and none of your common brown ones."

On he strolled, lifting his legs more carefully than ever, and arching his lovely long neck.

"Watch your step, watch your step!" screamed an impudent magpie.

"Such manners!" retorted the Heron. "The manners, one might say — well, just the manners of a magpie."

Then he suddenly felt hungry; and no wonder. It must have been *forty minutes* since he had tasted a mouthful of food!

He made his way to the edge of the stream, and looked down into the clear water. What had become of the pike? Where could all the carp be? Where indeed? Instead he saw some little fish leaping high above the water. Alba the Heron gave them one contemptuous glance.

"Sunfish!" he sneered. "It looks to me as if this creek was pretty well fished out."

But pretty soon some gudgeon swam by; a fish not to be despised, and in sufficient numbers to make a hearty meal.

"I'm known as a *Heron* :
as such, I live high."

"Perhaps they think I'll eat *them*," said the Heron. "The next thing I know it will be a mess of *minnows*. I'm a Heron, I'd have you understand; and I wouldn't dull my bill on such as you if I had to stand here on one leg for a whole week."

The gudgeon swam quickly away — not minding in the least that the big bird had seemed a little rude to them.

But, whew! How hungry he was. He remembered how, earlier in the day, he had let a worm crawl away without touching it. If only that worm would turn up now!

Alas, it was too late. He, the Heron, who had had no appetite for carp, was forced at last to make his supper on — what do you suppose? On one fat Snail — and not a bite besides.

Which would seem to show that it does not always pay to be so particularly particular!

JOCKO THE MONKEY AND MOUSER THE CAT

JOCKO the monkey and Mouser the cat were on the best of terms. Jocko — who would hardly have been called handsome, even by his mother—greatly admired Mouser's good looks, and thought she was the most beautiful creature he had ever seen. Of course in some ways she was not so important as a monkey. She had no pouches in her cheeks, where nuts and other things could be hidden away, and eaten at one's convenience. Her tail, though prettily striped, was not of much use to her, and not at all to be compared with that of Jocko, who could curl *his* tail around the bar of a trapeze or the branch of a tree, and swing there at his pleasure.

On the other hand, she had lovely soft fur, trimmed underneath with white, pretty white paws on which she walked in the most graceful manner, and wonderful green eyes that glowed in the darkness like coals of fire.

Then, how she could purr! This gift in itself seemed an amazing one to Jocko, who could make no pleasant sound at all, but could only chatter like the monkey he was.

When they were all alone at night, in the big house where their master lived, Jocko would sit quietly — fascinated by Mouser's glowing green eyes that shone so in the dark, and listening with his ugly ears to her pleasant purring.

Perhaps it was that Mouser reminded Jocko of something he dimly remembered in his old home in Asia, where he had been captured when a mere baby. They called his home the jungle — a place so overgrown with trees and grass that a man can hardly make his way through it, but in which snakes and monkeys and tigers are quite at ease.

A tiger; that was it! Mouser reminded Jocko of a tiger. But a tiny, friendly tiger; not a terrible, savage one who would eat up a monkey at a mouthful. Yes, the Jungle might have been a pretty good place for a monkey to live in. But dodging tigers and snakes was a little hard on the nerves, while here in this comfortable house one could live like a lord, and without a stroke of work!

And Jocko was not straight from the Jungle. He had had another master first. This man was an organ-grinder. He put a funny little hat on Jocko's head, dressed him in a queer little long-skirted coat, and taught him to beg for pennies. It was not a pleasant life for an intelligent monkey to live; and Jocko, who really had brains and knew how to use them, looked anything but cheerful. The music itself that his master played on the wheezy old organ was rather dismal music. Even the waltzes he played, and the airs from the Italian operas, seemed sad and sleepy tunes as he ground them out; and yet not so sad as Jocko seemed to be. If anyone looks sadder than a sad monkey, with a chain around his waist, and a comical cap worn a little on one side — well, we never happen to have seen anyone so sad, and we hope we never shall.

The chain around his waist did not improve Jocko's temper. It was always there to remind him that he could not run away, but must go on begging pennies for the rest of his life. A long cord was fastened to the end of this chain; and while his master held the other end of the cord, Jocko would sometimes be obliged to climb up the front of a house, clear to the second-story window, where some one was waiting with a penny or two. It was then that Jocko thought how easy it would be, were it not for the chain, to jump to the water spout, climb away up to the roof, and scamper off along the house-tops. If he could not get back to the jungle, he might at least escape to some park, and live there with the squirrels and pigeons. But it was no use. He would make a sly effort to bite through the chain; but it was too thick and strong. So down he would go again when his master tugged at the cord and scolded at him in Italian.

Then one blessed day his new master bought him. Bought him for a pet — just think of that! — and took him home to his big house, to keep company with Mouser.

It was some time before Jocko could get accustomed to being petted and made much of; but after a while he made himself quite at home; and the one danger now was that he would be badly spoiled. He had almost forgotten his sad life in the streets. But he had picked up some tricks and manners that are not pretty in a parlor; and his master was obliged to be patient with him, and to teach him how to behave. The monkey's new master was indeed almost *too* kind-hearted, and we fear that Jocko came to do pretty much as he pleased in many ways. After all, he was just a monkey, and monkeys are known all the world over for getting into all kinds of mischief.

His one great weakness was nuts; and these he would do anything to get. One night his master was expecting company; and as there was a big fire-place, with a bright fire burning, he thought his guests would enjoy some roasted chestnuts. So he placed them on the hearth, close to the hot coals; and then left the room on another errand.

Mouser was dozing by the fire, after drinking a saucer of cream; when in stole Jocko through the open door. At once he smelled the chestnuts, and made his way to the edge of the hearth. As the shells cracked and gave forth a tempting odor, his mouth watered. He *must* have those nuts. But, oh! how hot the fire was; and the big, flat fire shovel was much too clumsy for even him to manage. He thought a moment; then he looked at the cat. *He* admired *her* for her beauty; but she admired *him* just as much for his brains, and would do almost anything he told her.

"Come, Mouser," he said. "Come quick; or these chest-nuts will burn, and master would not like it."

Mouser arched her back, stretched herself, and came forward.

"Look!" said Jocko. "The nuts will be burned black; and I am so awkward I would only burn my fingers if I tried to save them. But you are as quick as lightning. Then, besides, wild animals are afraid of fire, and I have not ceased to fear it; while *you* are afraid of nothing. I don't know whether I admire you most because you are so beautiful, or because you are so brave. Just a quick jerk with your paw, and out the nuts will come. Hurry, Mouser. I just *know* you can do it!"

Jocko, you see, thought if he would pay the cat a few compliments, she would snatch the chestnuts from the fire for him, and *he* would not have to burn his fingers. And Jocko, it seems, was right. Mouser was so pleased with his praise that, quick as a flash, in went a paw and out came a chestnut. Jocko's only job was to *eat* them; and so clever was he at *that* sort of work that the last nut had been swallowed when his master returned.

But Jocko was not punished. His master merely looked at him, and shook his finger. And to Mouser he said:

"Poor, stupid kitty! Don't you know any better than to scorch your paws for chestnuts you never eat yourself?"

And ever since then, when any person is weak enough to do a tricky thing for another who does not dare do it himself — that person is called a cat's-paw!

44

So Mouser ~ pleased ~ sly
Jocko's wish obeyed.

THE GRAPES HANG HIGH FOR REYNARD THE FOX

IT HAD been a hard day for Reynard the fox. All through the night before the hounds had been running, and he had not dared to leave his hole. When he came out at last, in the early morning, and sniffed the air, his enemies had gone and the pleasant woods were safe. But the fox family was in need of food. The six little foxes, born in April, were as yet but five months old; it would be a whole year until they were really grown full size, and chasing their own tails was as much as could be expected of them at present. Mrs. Fox, the vixen, had turned hunter, too; so that Reynard with her help had kept the frolicsome cubs fat and well. But when both of them had to lie low all through the night, with only a few old bones to pick, dinner seemed far away indeed.

Bobby, the bad little fox, was on his worst behavior. He gnawed the last bit from his own bone, and then snatched his sister's share, and barked at her when she bit him. Sorrel, the surly little fox, was not much better. He always *was* hard to please, and growled and grumped if he did not have a chicken dinner at least once a week. And all he had had to eat since yesterday was just a few worms.

"I'm tired of worms, so I am!" he wailed. "If I don't get a partridge pretty soon, I'll go out and hunt for myself; and then maybe the hounds will get me —'n *then* you'll be sorry!"

"Stop your whining, Sorrel!" said Mrs. Fox. "You'd like your father to risk his life for a chicken just because you're too spoiled to eat some perfectly good worms. Now, don't let me hear another bark out of you, and I'll see if I can find you a fat beetle."

"A fat *beetle!*" grumbled Sorrel to himself. "Whoever heard of a *beetle* being *fat!*" Then he sat up and sucked his paws — just to show how badly abused he was.

So that is why Reynard the fox ventured out in the broad day. *Something* must be done.

Off he trotted, with his eye cocked and his ears wide open for whatever might be stirring in the woods. But the woods for once were without life of any sort — or so it seemed.

"It's a hard world for a fox," he murmured. "I never killed a sheep in my life, and I never sucked an egg. And there's old farmer Josh with two hound dogs I wouldn't trust alone with a lamb or a hen's nest. Talk about your hypocrites. It makes me sick!"

The fact is, he was feeling pretty blue — as one is apt to

"Those grapes are sour!"

be with an empty stomach and a dry tongue. Then all at once he stopped short. He had come to an old wall in the wild pasture — all that was left standing of a building gone to ruin; up this old wall grew a vine, and on the vine were: GRAPES.

Reynard was fond of fruit — and here was some much to his liking. Rosy bunches of grapes! Come to think of it, his own special fruit, called by his own name. *Fox grapes!* He looked up, and licked his chops. M-m-m — oh my!

Oh, my! But oh, how high! There they hung in great ripe clusters — and just beyond his reach. Once, twice, three times he jumped. Once, twice, three times he failed, and fell back.

Reynard stood there, with his tongue hanging out. For once he was defeated; but would he admit it? No, indeed! If he could not get a thing, why then he did not want it.

"Bah!" said he. "What a fool I am. Those grapes are sour. Let farmer Josh feed them to his pigs — poor things!"

And just how he got his breakfast the story does not say.

DAVY GREEN TRIES HIS NEW SLING

DAVY GREEN had made himself a new sling!
It was not an ordinary bean-shooter, with rubber-
bands and a forked stick, and a bit of soft leather
for the bean or buckshot. More than one boy in the village —
including Davy himself — had long possessed a sling of that
sort; and no doubt it is deadly enough. When the aim is
good — over goes some poor pigeon, or perhaps a song-bird;
and when the aim is bad — well, in that case the village
glazier has a job replacing somebody's broken window pane.

Sometimes it is much worse than a broken window pane.
One day Davy took a long chance, and let fly at a pigeon,
but hit the Deacon's horse instead. The Deacon's horse,
which was hitched to a buggy, and was dozing out in front of
the Deacon's house, had never been known to go faster than
a walk. But this time it woke up with a start, and went
loping down the street at a scandalous gait that brought everybody in the village to the windows; that is, to say, everybody
but grandfather Green, who could not *get* to the window
because of his rheumatism, and so missed an exciting time.

The exciting time for Davy came a little later on, when
the Deacon called to see grandfather Green. Something was
said about "sparing the rod and spoiling the child," and

grandfather Green agreed with the Deacon that it would be too bad to spoil Davy. So Davy, who had thrown away his sling when the horse ran off, did not get another one — and we must suppose the Deacon's ideas were carried out.

Now, Davy was not exactly what you would call a *bad* boy. In our opinion, the worst thing Davy did was to go around killing innocent birds with his sling. This he did whenever he got the chance; and if he killed more robins than were killed by the Deacon's boy, it was because his aim was better, and his sling was more carefully made. The truth is, in all the village there was only one boy who did not kill song-birds; and that was because he had been taught to love them, and to know their various songs and calls. Also, that to kill an inoffensive bird or beast just for the *pleasure* of killing was cruel and wicked. There is no fun in it. How would he like it if he were a bird? Not a bit — would he!

If Davy had been told this he might have mended his ways. Or if some one had made him a present of a book about birds, with pictures in many color, and made him understand how useful and beautiful they are, he would have seen how mean and silly it was to take a robin's life, or to wound a woodpecker who was trying to destroy the worms.

But no one gave Davy such a book, and no one told him these things; and when he got into trouble no one seemed to know any better cure than a whipping. Perhaps his looks were against him. His carroty red hair needed combing and cutting. His trousers were ragged — the collar gone from his shirt. He seldom wore shoes.

The worst of it was, the whippings Davy got did him no good. He seemed to forget he had been punished. Time passed, and Davy had forgotten all about the Deacon's horse. Summer was at hand, and the woods outside the village were his favorite playground. There he would wander with a fishing pole, or set up "Figure 4" traps in which he never caught anything, or "smoke out" squirrels that were always too spry for Davy's new sling.

Yes, as we said at the beginning — Davy had made him-self a new sling. And such a sling! Its like had never been seen before in the village. It was Davy's own idea. By this we do not mean that Davy *invented* the sling. We mean it was his own idea to make a sling like the one his Sunday school teacher told him about!

Fancy that! How could Miss Spencer imagine for a moment that when she coaxed Davy to come *just once* to her class he would get an idea from the lesson she never *meant* him to get. How could she know that when she told them the story of David and Goliath, and showed them the picture of little David slaying his big enemy with a *sling* —.

Now you see, don't you?— what Miss Spencer did *not* see. All *she* saw was Davy Green's face lighting up at the tale of that other David — Davy Green's eyes opening wide at the picture of the weapon that killed Goliath.

"Davy is not such a bad boy, after all," said dear Miss Spencer, dismissing the class. "I'm sure there's a great deal of good in him."

And so there was. But the goodness in Davy had not broken out. Not yet. The hopeful words had hardly left Miss Spencer's lips when Davy was hunting the leather and seeking the string that would make a sling like David's!

We should much prefer to tell you that Davy made a botch of it; or that having fashioned the sling he could not learn to use it. But there it is in the picture; and there is Davy with an ugly look on his face — his feet firmly planted, his hand outstretched to hurl the pebble that means death to the Dove.

Means death! But luckily, *meaning* to do it is *one* thing, and really *doing* it and doing it successfully, is quite another. The Dove was close at hand; in the sling was a smooth round pebble. "You'll make a pigeon-pie," the boy was saying under his breath. "Now!"

But at this moment something happened; and to under-stand just how and why it happened we must go back a few minutes to the time just before Davy came along with his new sling looking for something to kill.

A thirsty Ant had crawled to the edge of the brook, in order to get a drink. Then a little wave lapped the shore, and the Ant fell into the water. All in vain he struggled. To this small insect the brook seemed an ocean; it was only a matter of a few minutes till the poor creature would be drowned.

Luckily the Dove saw what had happened. Instead of trying to rescue the Ant with her bill, and thus perhaps injure him, the gentle bird quickly obtained a long stalk of grass. This she placed on the water, so as to make a bridge from the bank to the Ant, who crawled up on the grass stem, and thus reached the shore in safety.

"You have saved my life," said the Ant, "and I hope I may some time repay you."

The chance to do so was not long delayed. The Dove perched on a branch of an old tree near by; and the Ant had just dried himself, when along came Davy with his sling — almost stepping on the Ant as he stopped and took aim at the bird. Quick as he was, the Ant was even quicker; and stung him on the heel.

"Ouch!" he cried; and the Dove, alarmed by his cry, flew away.

Davy saw the Ant, and tried to kill him; but the Ant crawled away under a big rock. The Ant's sting pained him so that he hopped around on one leg, lost his balance, and fell

AMOR  VINCIT

Said he,
"You'll make a pigeon-pie."

sprawling on the hard ground. Then the Deacon's boy came along, and began to laugh. *Perhaps* he had heard how Davy happened to make his new sling. Davy now threw it at him, but it fell into the water and was lost. And, for some reason he did not explain, Davy never made another.

People who kill for the pleasure of killing are uneducated — that's the kindest way to describe them — they don't know any better! When we know better we appreciate the birds and beasts — appreciate the odds they have and what a really beautiful job they make of life. Uneducated people are people who do not think. They never consider the other fellow — don't know Jesus said "love thy neighbor as thyself," and that birds and animals are often the nicest neighbors we have.

HOW LEO THE LION WAS KILLED BY THE GNAT

LEO the Lion — King of all the Beasts — was in a bad temper; and all because of Reynard the Fox.

The Lion, it seems, had long been asked to listen to many complaints as to Reynard's ill behavior. Fang, the Wolf, who was jealous of Reynard, complained that the Fox was driving all the Rabbits out of the country. Not only did he eat more than his own share, but he drove the Rabbits from their holes — being too lazy to dig a hole for himself. Worse still, he was not satisfied with *one* hole, but pretended that he needed two or three of them, into which he could run and hide when the hounds were too hot on his trail. "Pretty soon," said the Wolf, "there will not be enough Rabbits to go around — and all because Reynard is so *greedy*. If there's one thing I dislike more than another in an animal, it's *greediness*."

It was rather funny to hear a Wolf talk like that; and the Lion might not have paid much attention to him. But along came Chanticleer the Cock, who complained that Reynard had stolen three of his finest Hens; along came Mouser the Cat, who complained that Reynard made away with all the Mice; and along came Baldy the Vulture, who complained that Reynard had taken the food the Lion had left for *him*.

Finally, along flew the Raven, who complained that Reynard had cheated him out of a large lump of cheese! And this at least we know was really the case.

The long and short of it was that Reynard was put on trial for being a thief; and when the trial took place, so many enemies of the Fox were on hand that they made a strong case against him, and Reynard was declared guilty and condemned to die!

But Reynard had not forgotten how to use his tongue; and no one could put on such a penitent face. He seemed so sorry for the things he had done, and so determined to lead a better life, that the Lion actually agreed to let him go. And that night the laughing Hyaenas laughed louder and longer than ever.

"What were those Hyaenas laughing at?" said the Lion to the Magpie, the next morning.

As he could easily fly away, the Magpie did not fear the King of Beasts.

"They were laughing," answered the Magpie, "at the way the Fox fooled you. The Fox was not one bit sorry. Any one but a Lion would know that a Fox is foxy."

At this the Lion flew into a rage. And being in a bad temper, his judgment was bad, too; so that when a Gnat buzzed along and bit him, he made a terrible swipe with his paw, but only succeeded in tearing a hole in his own face.

"Miserable insect!" roared the Lion. "Do that again, and I'll smash you flat!"

"Indeed!" said the Gnat. "Did you never see me sting an Ox? And an Ox weighs a lot more than you do. Just catch me if you can!"

Again he stung the Lion — again and again; and each sting drew blood. In vain the King of Beasts laid about him with his great paws; in vain he lashed his tail, and roared till the very hills shook with the sound. Each time he struck at the Gnat he struck himself; until at last he was weak with many wounds, and lay stretched out on the ground.

"If you meddle with me
I will not guarantee that you
won't be slammed perfectly flat."

"Bzz-zz!" said the Gnat as he flew away. "That will teach you to pick on one of your own size!"

But he, too, had bragged a bit too soon. The next moment he had flown into a spider's web; and there, we fear, we must leave him.

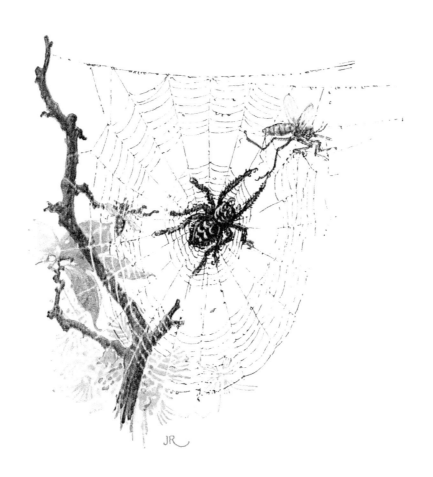

THE STORK GETS EVEN WITH REYNARD THE FOX

THE Raven never forgave Reynard the Fox for taking his cheese; and he never missed a chance to show him up. One day he met Mistress Stork, looking at herself in a pool and fussily arranging her feathers. The Raven really envied birds with brighter colors than his own. "The giddy old thing!" he muttered to himself. Then, aloud, he asked politely: "Are you engaged this evening, Mistress Stork?"

"Not exactly *engaged*," giggled Mistress Stork. "One could hardly be engaged to a *four-footer*—could one? But I am engaged *to dine* with a rather gay gentleman. Perhaps you know him — Mr. Reynard the Fox, Esquire."

"I know him, all right enough," croaked the Raven. "And all I can say is — *you* watch out. Specially if he asks you to *sing!*"

"*Me* sing?" said the Stork — quite forgetting her grammar. "Whoever heard of a Stork *singing*, I'd like to know." ·

"Just the same," quoth the Raven, sadly, "he's apt to ask you. And don't you do it — whether you can or not."

"I promise," she agreed, giving a last touch to her plumage. "And now I must be flying, or the soup will be cold."

61

"One thing more," croaked the Raven, as Mistress Stork mounted high into the air. "If he offers you *cheese*, don't you take it from him. It's stolen! You *hear* me? S-t-o-l-e-n — stolen!"

"Poor old Raven!" said Mistress Stork as she flew along. "Oh, well! It takes all kinds of birds to make a world."

Pretty soon she reached the place where Reynard was to entertain her. There he was; and there was the steam from the soup. How good it smelled to a hungry bird — who knows that soup is something special extra, and seldom served except on Leap Year, and not even then if it rains or snows!

"This is summer soup," said the Fox, with his most fascinating wink. "Summer soup always simmers. If you like simmering soup, *I* say serve it in the summer."

The Stork smiled. How witty Mr. Reynard was!

"You won't mind," continued the Fox, "if I tell you it's bird's-nest soup, made from the nests of birds — *present company excepted*. It comes from China — so it's *served* on china, according to the custom of the Chinese. And as I have broken my best bowl, I have put it all on one big plate. Pray help yourself!"

Mistress Stork stared. *How* was she to help herself from a *flat* plate, when her beak was so very long? With her worst table manners she could get but a drop or two.

"Don't be backward," said the Fox, pretending not to notice her plight. "The French people say that a plate should be licked clean."

All the time his long tongue was busy, lapping up the soup, while Mistress Stork barely got a beakful. Yet the shrewd bird made no complaint.

"I hope you'll excuse me, but I'm not feeling as peckish as I might," she said. Too much gravel in my luncheon to-day, I'm afraid. But I *do* enjoy seeing *you* eat. You do it so *thoroughly*, if you know what I mean."

Pretty soon the Fox had gobbled up all the soup, and licked the plate so clean that washing it would be an easy job.

Father Fox was invited
to eat from an urn.

"That's the way he does *his* housekeeping," remarked Mistress Stork to herself. Then she said to the Fox:

"It's been such a treat to dine with you. I wish *I* had your sense of humor. No wonder all the animals are envious. Now, when can you come and sup on soup with *me?* Suppose we say Saturday."

Reynard was a bit surprised that the Stork bore him no grudge; but he was promptly on hand at the place and hour appointed. When, however, he beheld the "soup plate," his eyes bulged; for, before him stood an *urn*, with a long neck — little above and big below. "I hope you admire my urn," said Mistress Stork, without cracking a smile. "It's a genuine Grecian urn, and the soup is genuine vermicelli soup, made with the most *delicious* worms, imported especially from *Angle-terre* — which is French for *England*, as you probably know. One does *so* adore the French style of cooking. And for an extra flavor, I have stirred it with the tail of a Fox—*present company always excepted.*" He looked at the tall vase — much too deep for his tongue; and then he looked at Mistress Stork with a wry face. The Fox trotted off without a word — his tail between his legs. For once he had met his equal — if she *was* a mere Stork!

THE ASS WHO PUT ON THE SKIN OF A LION

EVERYBODY in the village agreed that old Martin was *wise*.

"You can't fool old Martin," they used to say. "You can't pull the wool over *his* eyes. Old Martin *has cut his eye-teeth*."

Which was quite true in more ways than one.

You might suppose that if Martin were really as wise as they said he was, he would have made more money in all the years he had lived. Instead of dressing in a smock and hobnailed shoes, you might think he would have managed to get garments more worthy of a wise man.

But the simple truth is, that Martin thought money was not so important as some other things. And as for clothes — he worked in a mill where they made meal; his clothes were suited to his work, and Martin liked work, and did it always in the best possible manner.

Besides being wise, Martin was happy. The two things seemed to go together in his case. He was wise in being happy, and happy in being wise.

Most people respected old Martin's opinions, and listened with attention to what he had to say. But of course there were exceptions, and one of these exceptions was Giles, the green-grocer's boy. Giles was lazy and discontented, and was always complaining because other people had more than *he* had. He liked to talk better than he liked to work; and if he found some one to listen, he would stop on his way to a customer, with a wheelbarrow laden with vegetables, and argue for an hour at a time.

"Brains don't get you anywhere," he would say. "If you want to succeed you've got to *advertise* yourself. Keep on tellin' people how smart you are, and after a while they'll believe you. There's more than one man in this town who's got rich just by pretendin' he's a sight more than he is. It's just pretendin', I tell you — just pretendin', that makes people take off their hats to you."

At this kind of talk old Martin would shake his head.

"Try working hard for a change," he would say to Giles. "And *you* take my word for it, son — pretendin' to be what you are *not*, don't carry you very far. It may go for a while with *some* people; but sooner or later you'll be found out for just what you *are*, my boy!"

"Bah!" said Giles. "I tell you it's just *lookin'* like you were big! That's what counts every time in *this* world."

Hardly had he spoken, when shouts were heard. Men and women ran by, or hid themselves in doorways. They acted just as if a wild beast were after them. Then came the cry:

"Lion, Lion! Look out for the Lion!"

"No lion has that
long and hairy ear!"

Giles stopped talking, and looked down the street. The next moment he turned, with a sudden movement that upset his wheelbarrow; and took to his heels.

"It's a Lion!" he yelled, louder than all the rest!

Old Martin was the only one who did not lose his head. "Africa is a long way off," he said to himself; "and there's no circus showing in town. I wonder what it can be all about!"

He went to the door, looked out; and saw what really seemed to be a Lion coming along. A Lion? But who ever saw a Lion with two tails? And who ever saw a Lion with long, hairy ears? Old Martin laughed.

"Why, bless me!" said he. "If it isn't the Miller's own Ass! Some one has been playin' a trick, dressin' him up in that Lion's skin nailed on the tannery door. Well, *some* people are easy taken in!"

He put a noose around the Ass's jaws, and led him away.

"I wonder where Giles is gone," he chuckled. "I'd like to give him a proper introduction to this Ass!"

THE GRASSHOPPER GOES TO THE ANT

"IN THE good old sum-mer time — in the good old sum-mer time!" . . .

It was Gogo, the great green Grasshopper; and that was the song he sang.

These words, to be sure, may not be the *exact* words. Somehow or other, singers sing so queerly! They do not open their mouths, or they open them too wide, or they forget the words, or mispronounce them; and in any case you cannot be sure just what the song is about.

However, if these words are not the exact words that Gogo sang it is certain that what he sang sounded very much like them. When a singer sings in French or Russian, it's hard enough to understand; but when he sings in the *insect language*, it takes seven learned men, wearing large spectacles, and with ear-drums on their ears, and working hard day and night, including the Fourth of July, to tell one chirp from another.

That's the reason why insect language and insect music are so wonderful. You cannot learn them out of books; but must go into the fields for yourself, and listen and listen. Why, it took all of five hundred years, if not more, to find out just what the Grasshopper said to the Ant, and the Ant said

69

to the Grasshopper — as told in this very story; and so you will understand why the words of Gogo's song were so difficult to translate into ordinary English.

At any rate, the song was about summer. Of that you may be quite sure. Nor can anybody deny that he sang it all summer long, accompanying himself with the harp he carries on his hip, underneath his wing.

Gogo was a born musician; and when one is a born musician one is bound to sing or play much of the time — whatever may be the consequences. So Gogo sang all summer in the pleasant fields; while all around him the Ants toiled and toiled, and ran around like mad, and sometimes behaved quite as if they had lost their heads.

At least, Gogo, in his careless way, thought as much. The trouble was, *he did not understand Ants.* All that Gogo knew or cared to know was *music.* The Ants, also, were interested in only one thing; and that one thing was *work,* for which Gogo had no talent at all, and never had been taught to do. It was not his fault, you see; but simply the way he was made, and his lack of a good common school education.

Then summer fled, and winter was at hand. Gogo was hungry and cold. Where could he warm himself, and who would lend him food?

"I'll ask one of the Ants," said Gogo, hopefully. "I know a maiden Ant named Miranda. *She'll* help me."

In a mound of earth and leaves was the door to her winter quarters; and in he went. He found Miranda still hard at

"He who will not work, shall not eat"

"Lend me food and I vow
I'll return it."

work — churning away with one pair of hands and knitting a nightcap with the other. On the shelves were jars of honey-dew; on the floor were barrels and bags of grain.

"I'm hungry," said Grasshopper, briefly; "and I haven't a single red cent. Could you — er — accommodate me with the loan of a little food? I'll pay you back next June."

Miranda the maiden Ant paused not a moment in her twofold toil.

"You do look kind o' down and out," she said. "Sure 'tain't all your own fault? What were you workin' at in the summer?"

"Working at?" echoed Grasshopper in an injured tone. "I was cultivating my voice. Didn't you hear me? I *sang* all through the summer."

"You *sang* all summer?" said Miranda the maiden Ant, with a sneer. "So you *sang*, eh? Then no doubt you can dance, too. Just hop away from here on those lanky old hind legs — and *dance* a bit for your bread. Hop along, I say!"

And Gogo hopped along. He could not help himself.

THE MILLER, HIS SON AND THE ASS

FOR several days people in the village talked of nothing else but how the Miller's Ass, dressed in the skin of a Lion, had scared everybody from the streets. It was not the Miller's fault, and not the fault of the Ass, that some one had played this trick; but it made an excuse for gossip, and idle tongues started the story that the Miller was to blame. Greatly annoyed by this gossip, the Miller at last said to his son:

"I've decided to sell the Ass at the Fair, and buy a horse instead; and then in time people will forget this thing ever happened."

So off they started for the neighboring town; and *the way* they started made everyone stare. The Miller was a kind-hearted man, and the Ass had long been a faithful servant, bearing heavy burdens without complaint. No animal is more patient and enduring than an Ass when he is well treated.

"He's borne big loads for *us*, all these years," said the Miller; "and now it's only right that we should carry *him*."

So they slung him on a pole, heels up; and you may be sure it was not very long until this manner of taking an Ass to market aroused the laughter of passers-by.

"How silly!" exclaimed one of these critics. "Tell me, if you can, *who* is the greatest Ass of those three."

At this the Miller grew red in the face. Then he unslung the Ass from the pole, set it on its feet, and bade his son get on its back, while he himself trudged alongside. But even this sensible arrangement did not please the people they passed on the road.

"What's the world coming to," said one, "when a strong young man rides, while his father is made to walk? Young people are selfish enough nowadays, without encouraging them to take no thought at all of their elders."

"It's much easier for the Ass to let the boy ride," answered the Miller; "but it may be, of course, that I am setting a bad example."

Saying this, he motioned to his son to get down, and climbed to the saddle himself. Then, pretty soon three young girls came along; and one of them began to giggle.

"Will you look at *that!*" she remarked. "Poor boy, limping along in the dust! It's easy to see he's half lame; while that old fellow sits there like a bishop, and lets him walk."

"Saucy girl!" muttered the Miller. Yet he did not wish her to think him unkind. "Get up here in front of me, Son," he said.

In this way they jogged on for a mile — the sturdy little beast making no fuss at all under such a heavy burden. But presently they met a man who called out:

"You'll kill that Ass if you're not careful. *I* call it cruelty to animals!"

"I'm afraid you're right," answered the Miller; "but I don't seem to be able to please anybody, no matter what I do."

The father and son now decided to walk, while the Ass marched proudly ahead. But in a few minutes they met two men, one of whom said to the other: "Look at them, wearing out their shoes, when they have an Ass to ride. *Three* Asses, *I* should say."

The way that they started
made everyone stare.

At this the Miller lost all patience.

"When you try to please everybody," he cried, "you please nobody.   From now on, I intend to please myself."

Which was, as it turned out, the most sensible thing he could do.

FERDINAND THE FROG DOES SOMETHING BIG

EVER since he was a tiny tad, Ferdinand the Frog had been rather spoiled by his parents.

They began by boasting about him, soon after he was hatched.

"Our Ferdinand," they would say, "is already so wonderful. Here he is hardly three months old, and shedding his tail. Isn't he cute? See him catch that fly with his tongue!"

However, nothing much might have happened had they not named him Ferdinand. It was this that proved to be his undoing, and altered the whole course of his life. With so many names to choose from — such as Jonathan, Rollo, or Percy, it may seem strange that his parents picked out the worst one. At least it was the worst for Ferdinand, who was made to feel his importance at a time when little frogs should be seen, and not heard. No sooner did he actually receive the name than his behavior grew more and more unbearable.

Unless some one was looking at him all the time, and admiring the things he did, he would either sulk, or fly into a temper. His faithful sister watched him till her eyes bulged more than ever; but even then he was not satisfied.

"Did you see how far I jumped?" he would insist. "Would

you like to see how deep I can dive? Did you know I could croak the loudest of any Frog in the pond?"

One day he remarked to his sister: "My name is Ferdinand, and I was born to do something big. Just you wait and watch me. I don't know exactly what it is I am going to do. But it's something *big*, I say; and when I *do* it, believe me you'll hear something *crack!*"

Alas! Ferdinand spoke not wisely, but too well. He did do something big, and something did crack. But the thing that cracked was Ferdinand.

His loving sister seemed to see the fate in store for him.

"I wish you wouldn't talk like that!" she entreated. "You are much too ambitious. Could you not forget for a little time that your name is Ferdinand?"

"That's just *like* a girl," her brother answered, proudly expanding his chest till he was twice his natural size. "Girls never *are* named Ferdinand. If they *were*, they would see just how it is."

"See me puff!"

"But, anyway; don't blow yourself up so big," she said. "You frighten me."

To frighten anyone — if only his sister, was something that seemed to Ferdinand quite big in itself. Such flattery turned his head.

"Pooh!" said he, "that's nothing. If I really wanted to, and tried hard enough, I could make myself as big as the Ox. There comes the stupid old thing now. I'll just blow myself up, and frighten *him*."

He blew and puffed, and puffed and blew, till he looked a bit like a balloon. The Ox went on feeding.

"That will do, Ferdinand!" cried his sister. "If you stretch your skin like that it will be all *flabby*, and you'll look ever so *old* and *ugly*."

But Ferdinand did not hear her. With one final puff, he stretched his skin till it cracked. Ferdinand's body had burst, and what had once been Ferdinand was scattered in little bits.

And the Ox went on feeding.

THE CITY MOUSE AND THE COUNTRY MOUSE

A REALLY intelligent Mouse, when he means to settle down for a time, does not leave everything to chance. He looks about him a bit before he decides; spends a night here and a night there, and always keeps in mind the slogan: "Safety First!"

Sam the City Mouse had sampled a variety of apartments before he found one actually to his liking. It was the home of a bachelor — a prosperous young broker who never stayed in except when he was asleep, and that was only six hours a night. He was the thoughtful sort of man who will leave a large layer-cake on the table, and never count the crumbs. Best of all, he was not the kind of man that kept a Cat.

Easy living always agreed with Sam. His fur was softer, his eyes were brighter. He paid more attention to his whiskers and his nails, and chose his collars and ties with great care.

Of course, even at the best, a Mouse is never quite safe. Maids come, and put the cake away, and fuss around at what they call "cleaning up." Anything may happen, and you never can tell.

But Sam did not borrow trouble. He knew no woman would ever set a trap for *him*; and the Master did not mind a few mouse-tracks. *No* sort of living thing in a big city is quite free from danger.

"Suppose people *do* come poking around when you least expect them. I should *scurry!*" said Sam.

Then he got to thinking about his cousin Seth, the Country Mouse; and when he thought how hard Seth had to work for a few grains of wheat, it made Sam smile.

"How his eyes would stick out to see *this* little old home-sweet-home!" he said to himself. "Seth must be lonesome down there among the pumpkins and the woodpiles. I reckon I'll have to ask him up here for a week-end with *me.*"

So Seth was invited, and Seth came. Sam was there to take his carpet-bag and umbrella, and show him around the place.

"Small, but rather swell, *I* should say!" remarked Sam, with a wave of his paw. And now if you don't mind, I'm going to take off my collar and tie. When I eat cake, it seems to come clear up into the neck; and these collars *are* cramping, there's no denying."

"Why do you wear them, then?" asked Seth, who wore a loose green muffler for all occasions.

"Well," explained Sam. "Everybody that is anybody wears them. It kind of sets you apart from the mob, I suppose. And then if it's cleaning day, with nothing much to eat, you can always stay your hunger by licking the starch.

A knock was heard.

I suppose that's what starch must be for, though I never thought of it till this minute. But come on into the cake. A piece of the chocolate icing, or would you rather bore right in, same's you do back home?"

"Thank you," said Seth. "I reckon I'll just nibble around some, till I find what's most to my taste."

At that moment came a loud knock on the door.

Sam scampered to the floor, followed by Seth. They hid themselves in a corner, and waited, hardly daring to draw breath. Then Sam plucked up his courage.

"It's nothing," he said. "Some one just knocked by mistake. Now they're gone, and we can go and finish our meal."

But the Country Mouse looked around for his carpet-bag.

"Back to the farm for *me*, Cousin Sam," he insisted. "You live an easy life — that's true enough, with cake at all hours. But *my* life keeps me out in the open air, and I'm not so liable to choke to death with fright when I swallow a grain o' wheat. So long!"

And Seth made tracks for home.

THE CAT SHOWS THE FOX HER ONE BEST TRICK

SOMETIMES Mouser the Cat was tired of staying around the house, where everyone petted her, and one day was much like another. Mouser was so spoiled that she actually almost forgot *why* she was called Mouser. The fact is, her Mistress did not wish her to catch mice; and then besides, the house was so well kept that no mouse ever came into it.

However, when a Cat's family, as far back as one can remember, has made a reputation for catching mice, it is not so easy to forget it altogether. After all, though it's nice to have your fur stroked and to get a saucer of cream whenever you mew for it, it's not so much *fun* as prowling around out-of-doors and doing things your Mistress would never dream you were doing.

In other words, there were times when Mouser the Cat wanted *excitement* more than anything else; and when she wanted excitement, you could not have kept her at home with a piece of liver.

Mouser lived in the country; and that of course was a great advantage. Only a little way from the house were the fields and the forest; and in the fields and the forest you could see and hear more in an hour than you could see and hear in a month curled up on a rug in the house.

Mouser, you see, loved *adventure*. That was plain enough to anyone who saw her, with her back slightly arched, stalking along through the tall grass. You knew then that she was not just a house-cat, but a cousin to the wild creatures of the woods; and you would perhaps guess that at such times Mouser made friends with animals *never allowed near the house*.

It was really so. Mouser had made a friend of Reynard the Fox; and often they would walk for hours together — enjoying the scenery, and perhaps some other things they picked up on their way.

Mouser's friend, Reynard, was not, however, the very same Reynard we have heard so much about. He looked like him, and might easily have been taken for him at a distance; but actually he was only a cousin, and not nearly so clever as *our* Reynard.

Now Mouser, we must admit, was not too modest in her opinion of herself, and the Fox could not help knowing his own good points because he was so much admired by the ladies; and one day as they walked together they began to talk of these things — each one being inclined to brag.

The Cat had been telling the Fox how quick she was on her feet, and how she had no fear of any hound that ran.

"I suppose," she said, slyly, "that *running* is the thing *you* count on most."

"Pardon me," said the Cat,
"I can't be staying."

"I can run a little," answered the Fox, proudly. "But I have *a hundred tricks* besides. Pray, how many have you?"

"For myself," admitted the Cat, hunching her shoulders, "I have but the *one* trick. Yet I find that one trick to be quite enough."

At that moment a pack of fox-hounds burst into view — yelping and baying.

"See!" said the Cat. "This is *my* trick."

In two bounds she had reached a tree, up which she climbed in perfect safety as the pack tore by.

The Fox was less fortunate. *He* could not climb like the Cat, and the hounds were almost on him before he saw them — as the picture shows. We fear that we shall not see him again, and that the Cat was right: *One* trick may be better than one hundred — provided it be a *good* trick.

THE HEN THAT LAID THE GOLDEN EGGS

ONCE there was a Farmer known all the country round for the many fine hens he raised. He had little Bantams and big Plymouth Rocks, hens that were pure white, and handsome black hens. Besides all these were the common or barnyard hens that are not much to look at, but can scratch well for a living, and give a pretty good account of themselves when it comes to laying eggs.

But these eggs laid by the common hens were not much to his liking. They were good fresh eggs — as good to eat as any that were laid by the high-bred fowls on the farm. The trouble was, they were *brown*; and *because* they were brown, some fussy people would not buy them — though the color made no difference at all in the *taste*, which you might suppose was the one thing that really mattered in an egg.

As the brown eggs did not fetch so much money in the market as the white eggs, we cannot well blame the Farmer for despising the common hens that laid them. But this was not all. He was, we are sorry to say, a greedy man in more ways than one; and one of his greedy ways was to think too much of money, and to think too little of the people on the farm who had to be fed. No one on that farm had ever eaten a white egg. No matter how well the hens were laying, or what a small price the eggs might fetch at certain seasons because they were so plentiful, nobody was allowed to eat a white one. If there were brown eggs enough to go around, well and good; and if there were *not* — well, in that case his family and the farm hands could eat what the ducks laid — or go without. If Jimmy, the chore boy, as much as *looked* at a white egg, it was enough to put the Farmer in a rage.

Thus it was that Jimmy did what he could to keep the common hens fat and satisfied. He fed them any extra crumbs that came his way, and he worked over-time to keep their houses fresh and clean; and the last thing at night he made sure the door was shut and fast, in case Reynard the Fox should come prowling around.

Jimmy was always up before daylight, to milk the cows; and he seldom finished his chores till long after dark. But no matter how much he had to do, he never neglected the common hens, and never neglected to gather all their eggs.

This in itself was no easy task. The common hens who had to scrtach for a living made their nests in all sorts of places. Sometimes they laid their eggs in the nice, clean nests Jimmy prepared for them; but often as not they would lay them in a fence corner, or in the wagon shed, or away up in the hay loft where only one who knew hens might suppose a hen would go. What made it harder was that nobody can ever tell whether a hen happens to be laying or not; and you cannot always be sure unless you watch her and see what she may be up to.

Jimmy had had his eye for a long time on one hen in particular. Hens have ways of their own; and this hen had a way of laying her eggs in the most unexpected places. Then she stopped laying altogether; and it was Jimmy's job to try to find out when she would begin again.

One day, after he had looked everywhere, as he thought, and had gathered all the brown eggs to be found — a Cock began to crow, and the hens began to cackle. Jimmy took another long look. Just as he suspected, the hen he had

90

The meanest of men.

watched so long was nowhere to be seen. At last he came where a ladder was propped against the side of a hayloft; so up the ladder he went, and there, sure enough, was the hen, with a large yellow egg in plain sight, and looking around her as if to say: "Well, what do you think of that!"

What Jimmy thought was: "I've earned that big egg, and I'll just have it for my breakfast — hard-boiled, to make it more hearty." So, the next morning he cooked it himself, and put it on the table. It was the biggest, yellowest egg he had ever seen.

Crack! Jimmy struck the egg sharply with his knife; but it did not break. A second and a third time he struck it; but all in vain. He might just as well have struck a stone.

"Hand it here!" said the Farmer, who was watching him. "I'll show you how!"

He took the egg, and brought it down on the table with a crash. But he only hurt his hand, while the egg was as sound as ever. Greatly excited, he got up; and going to the window, held the yellow thing up against the sun. The next moment he cried out:

"Where did you get this egg, you young rascal?"

Jimmy told him, and the Farmer's eyes shone with greed. Then, without another word, he rushed from the house.

Weeks passed. The Farmer now cared for this common hen as if she were worth her weight in gold; and indeed she was — for each day she laid an egg, and the egg was golden. Still he was not satisfied. Jimmy could hear him muttering to himself. "It's not enough, it's not enough!" he was saying.

Jimmy wondered what it meant. Then he saw the Farmer, with an axe in one hand and the hen in another, go quickly to the chopping block; and the next moment he had chopped off the poor hen's head.

"What is *one* egg a day?" Jimmy heard him saying. "I want *all* — all the gold that's inside her!"

But there *was* no gold inside her. Only the eggs were gold, and the Farmer in his greed had killed the hen that laid them!

The End

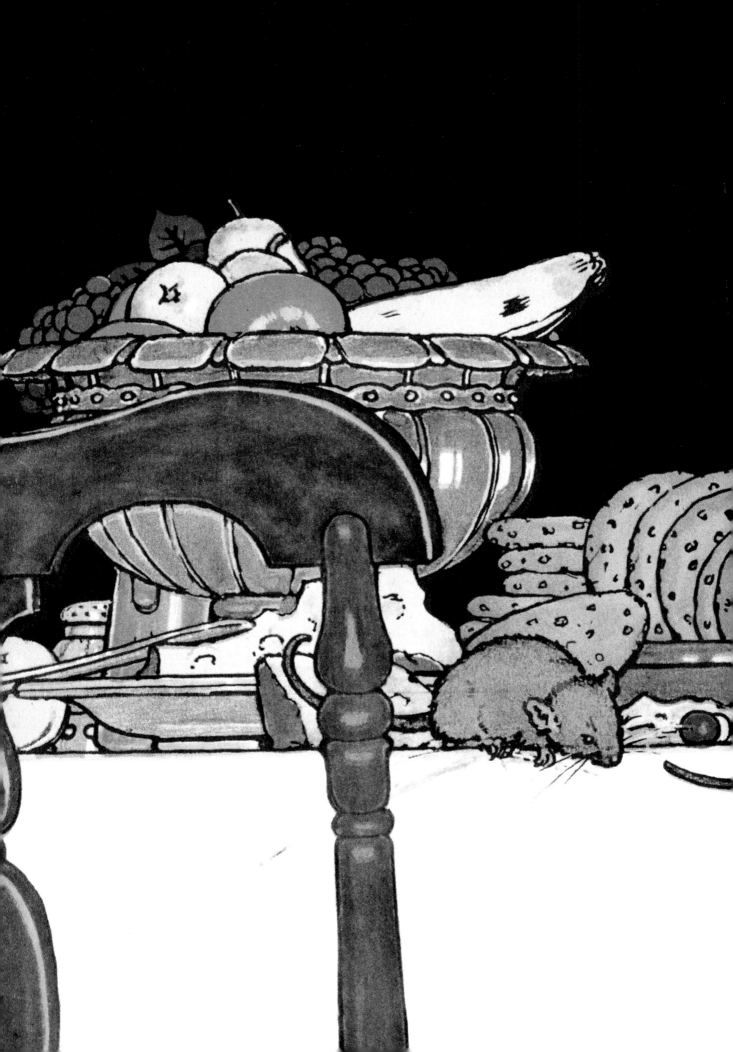